1

Mrs Mayblossom who lives at number 12 Fox River Road loves Christmas.

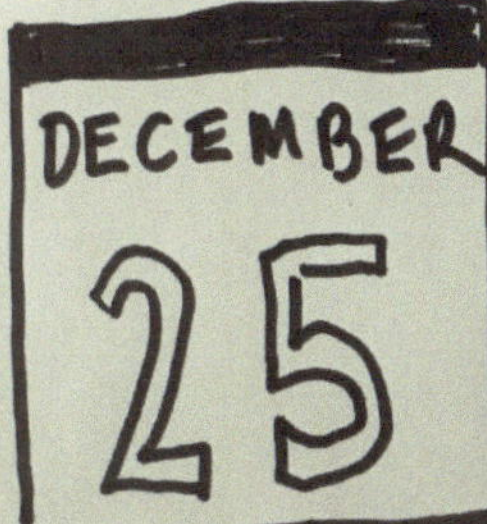

On November 25th Mrs Mayblossom gets very excited. Only 4 weeks to go.

Mrs Mayblossom
begins putting
up the Christmas
Tree.

4.

She then finds all the tree decorations

There are baubles, tinsel and the star that sits on top of the tree.

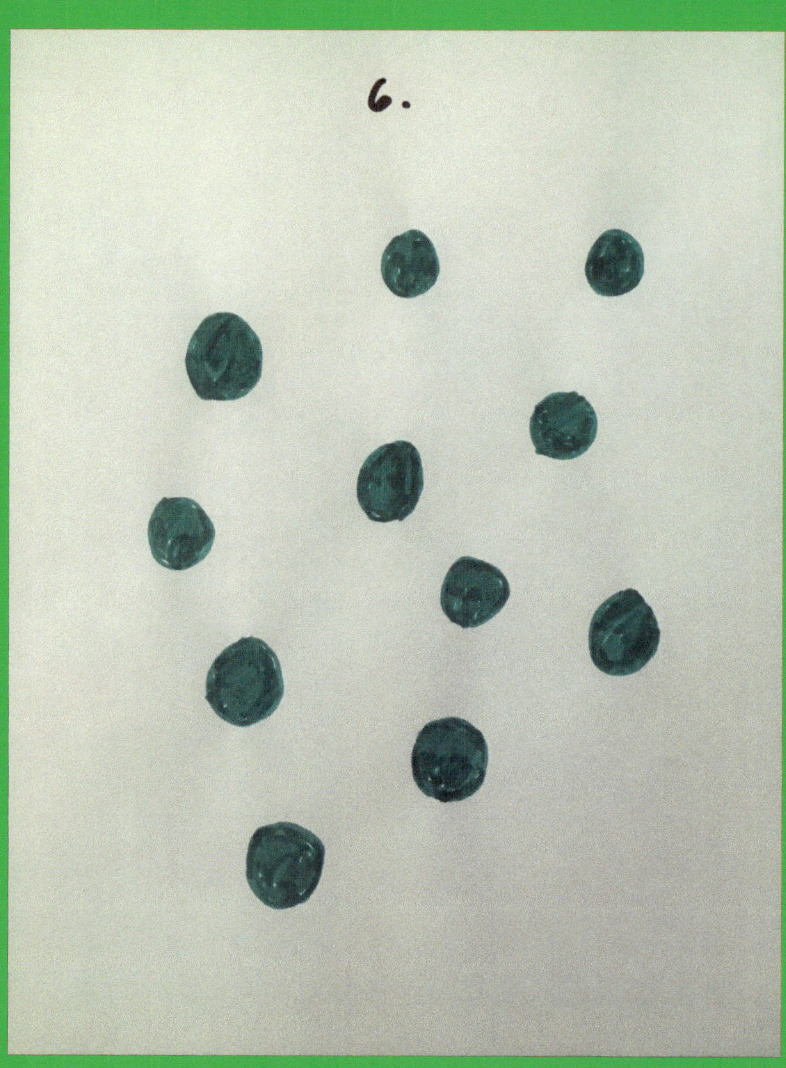
6.

7.

There are green baubles.

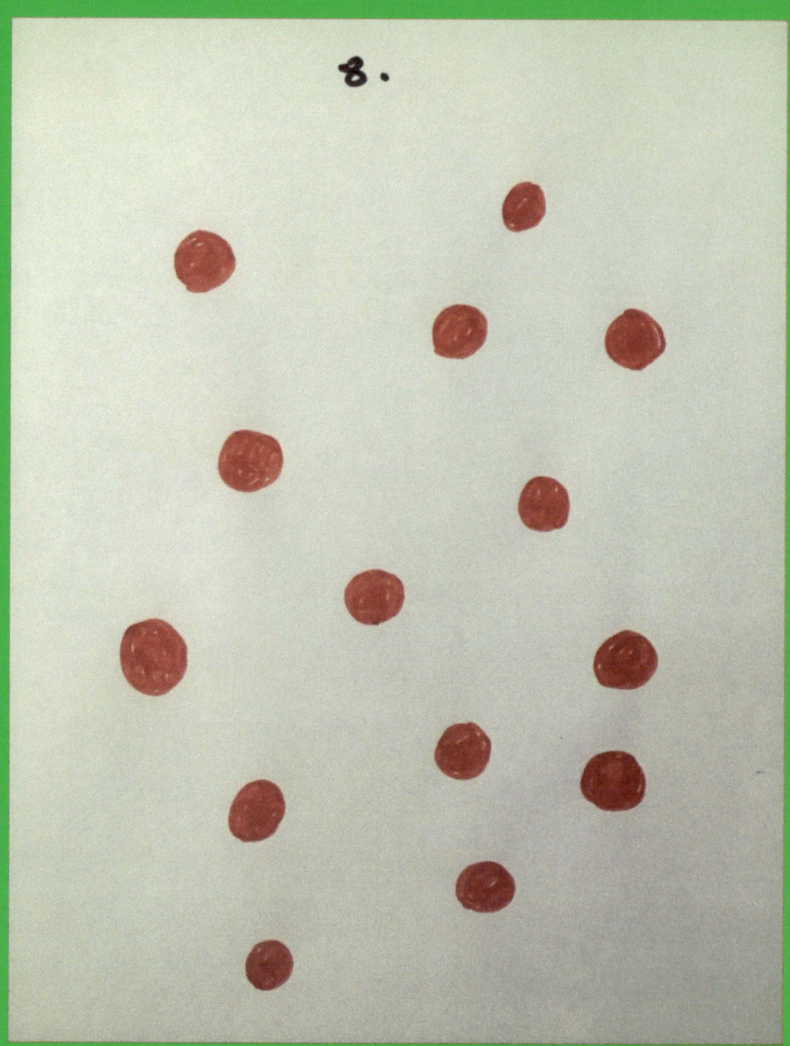
8.

9.

There are

red baubles.

10.

Lots of gold tinsel.

12.

13.

Finally, the big Gold star to go on top of the tree.

14.

Now with the
tree done
Mrs Mayblossom
puts the Christmas
wreath on the
front door.

16.

Mrs Mayblossom makes some sausage rolls on Christmas Eve. Her special recipe.

18.

19.

She listens to Christmas Carols on Christmas eve while she wraps presents.

20.

21.

It's Christmas Day!
Mrs Mayblossom
cooks a Turkey.

23.

24.

Some Yorkshire puddings.

25.

Some

Green

Beans.

Some roasted pumpkin.

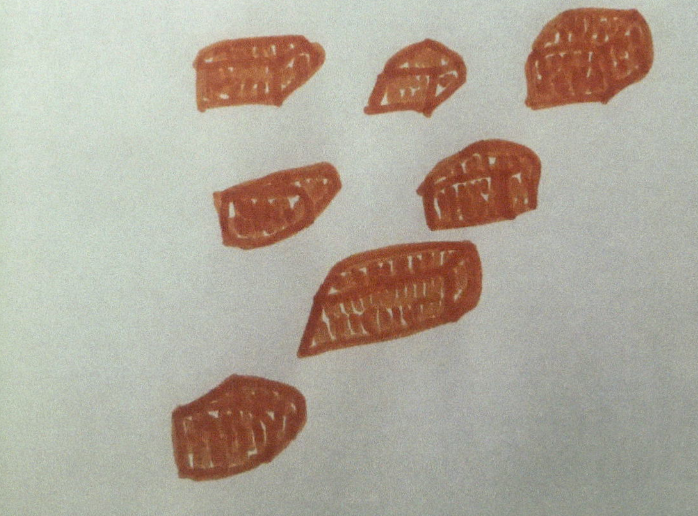

Gravy.

28.

A

Ham.

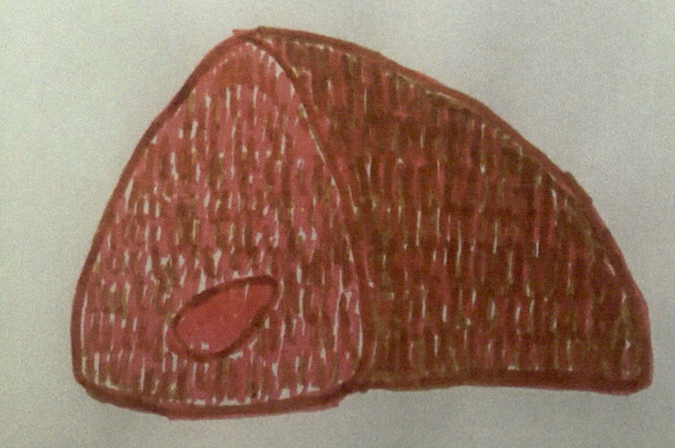

30.

Christmas Pudding.

31.

Don't forget
the
Bon Bons!

32.
LOVE
JOY
PEACE
FAMILY
HOPE
FRIENDS

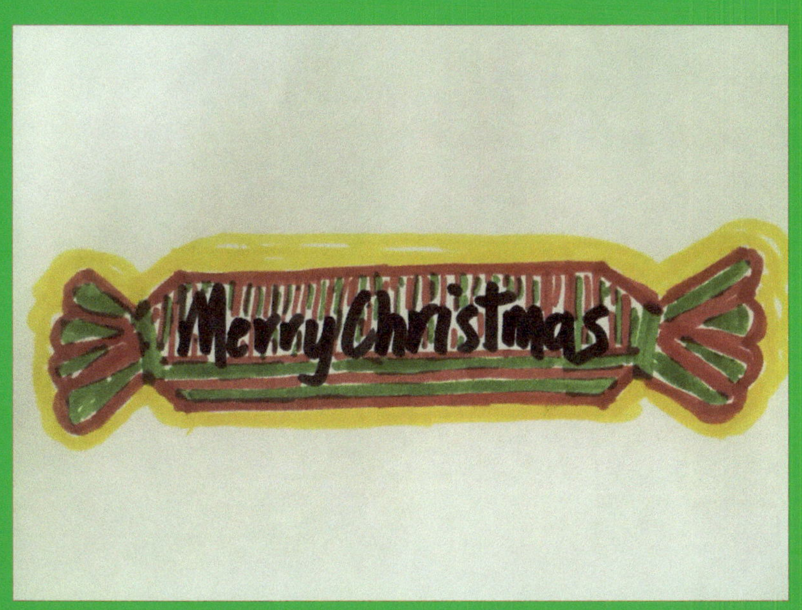
Merry Christmas

www.ingramcontent.com/pod-product-compliance
Ingram Content Group UK Ltd.
Pitfield, Milton Keynes, MK11 3LW, UK
UKHW060406300726
14090UKWH00006B/461

* 9 7 9 8 5 8 2 8 6 9 2 4 5 *